SPACE TRAVELERS

SeaStar Books · San Francisco

Front cover photograph: Space Shuttle Atlantis launches on mission STS-106
Title page photograph: Apollo 9 pilot David R. Scott stands in the open hatch of
the Command Module nicknamed "Gumdrop"

This book is dedicated to the brave men and women who have
lost their lives in the exploration of space.

Special thanks to reading consultant Dr. Linda B. Gambrell, Director, School of Education,
Clemson University. Dr. Gambrell has served as President of the National Reading Conference
and Board member of the International Reading Association.

Permission to use the following photographs is gratefully acknowledged:
front cover, 16–17, 34–35: courtesy NASA Human Spaceflight; title page, pages 2–3, 7, 8–9, 10,
12–13, 18–19, 20–21, 30–31, 36–37, 38–39, 40–41, 48, back cover: courtesy Great Images in NASA;
pages 4–5, 14–15, 25, 26–27, 33: courtesy Lyndon B. Johnson Space Center, NASA; pages 22–23,
26–27: courtesy Marshall Space Flight Center, NASA; 28–29: © Margaret Miller; pages 42–43,
46–47: courtesy Goddard Space Flight Center, NASA; pages 44–45: courtesy Jet Propulsion
Laboratory, NASA.

SeaStar is an imprint of Chronicle Books LLC.

Library of Congress Cataloging-in-Publication Data available.

Distributed in Canada by Raincoast Books
9050 Shaughnessy Street, Vancouver, British Columbia V6P 6E5

10 9 8 7 6 5 4 3 2 1

Chronicle Bools LLC
85 Second Street, San Francisco, California 94105

www.chroniclekids.com

People have always dreamed of ways to go into space. One story written 300 years ago told of a flock of wild geese pulling a man to the moon. More than a century ago, Jules Verne wrote a tale of a journey to the moon in a shell fired by a giant cannon. In 1961, the first human being was launched into space by a rocket.

Since then, hundreds of other men and women have traveled into space. Truly, we all live now in the space age.

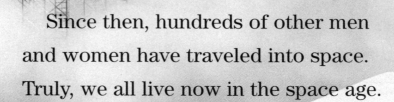

Rocket ships that can travel into space were developed in the 20th century. Today, more than 100 of these rockets are launched every year. Spaceships have only explored a small part of our solar system. No one from Earth has ever traveled into outer space beyond the moon, to the planets, or between stars and galaxies.

"Space" begins where Earth's atmosphere ends, but there is no exact boundary. The atmosphere is the blanket of air that protects us from the heat of the sun and the cold of space. One hundred miles above the surface of Earth, the atmosphere is almost gone.

Blasting off the ground with a rocket is the only way we know to get into space. We can't use an airplane, because its wings need air to lift the plane and its engines run on fuel that burns in air. A rocket moves by burning fuel and sending hot gases through an exhaust opening at its bottom. The force of the exhaust pushes the rocket off the ground.

Big rockets have three sections, or stages. When each stage uses up its fuel, it falls away to make the rocket lighter. Smaller rockets, called boosters, sometimes assist a first-stage rocket in takeoff. Each stage is smaller than the one before. When the third stage is dropped, the rocket's nose opens and a satellite or spaceship continues the journey.

Scientists needed to make sure that animals could live in space safely before humans were allowed to go there. On September 20, 1951, the former Soviet Union launched a rocket with a monkey and 11 mice inside the nose. This flight did not go into orbit, however. It was more like a very fast elevator ride. All of the animals survived the flight.

A chimpanzee named Ham was launched into space just before the astronaut Alan Shepard, Jr., went into space in 1961. Another chimp, Enos, spent three hours in flight before John Glenn's orbital flight in 1962. The list of animals that have gone into space includes rats, dogs, frogs, fish, ants, spiders, snails, beetles, and jellyfish.

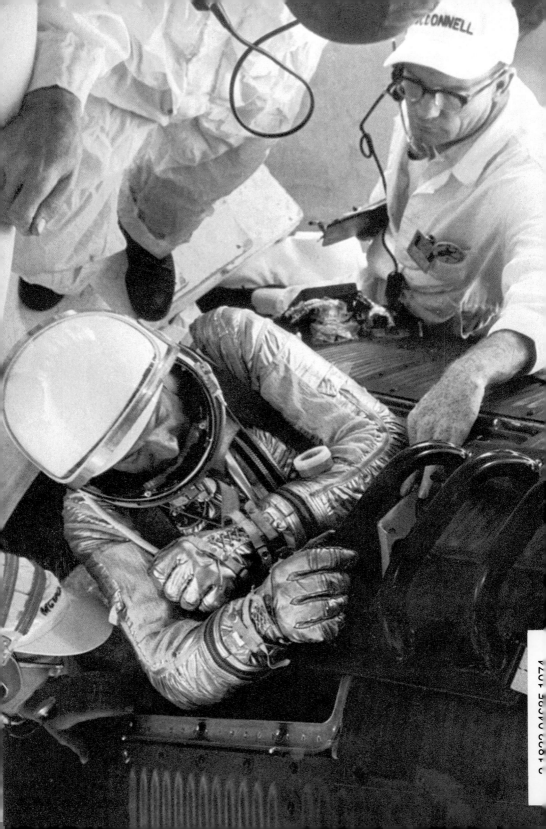

On April 12, 1961, Yuri Gagarin of the former Soviet Union became the first human to orbit Earth. He orbited once around Earth aboard Vostok 1 and experienced weightlessness for 89 minutes.

Several weeks later, the National Aeronautics and Space Administration (NASA) sent up the first United States astronaut aboard the Freedom 7 Mercury spacecraft. Alan Shepard flew for 15 minutes and came down safely in the ocean. After Shepard, America's first astronauts completed solo flights of up to two days. They flew in capsules that were about the size of a telephone booth.

The first United States space walk came during the Gemini mission on June 3, 1965. Four years after the first space walk, people would walk on the moon.

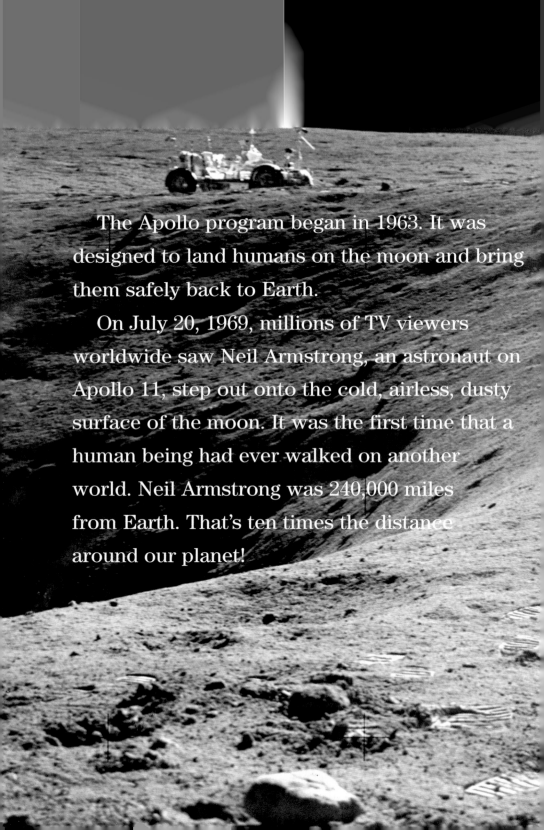

The Apollo program began in 1963. It was designed to land humans on the moon and bring them safely back to Earth.

On July 20, 1969, millions of TV viewers worldwide saw Neil Armstrong, an astronaut on Apollo 11, step out onto the cold, airless, dusty surface of the moon. It was the first time that a human being had ever walked on another world. Neil Armstrong was 240,000 miles from Earth. That's ten times the distance around our planet!

Eleven Apollo flights to the moon were launched between 1968 and 1972. The Apollo spacecraft were made up of three parts: a Saturn V Moon Rocket, a Command and Service Module (CM), and a Lunar Module (LM).

The Saturn V was the largest rocket ever launched. At 365 feet high, it was 60 feet higher than the Statue of Liberty and weighed 13 times as much. Most of the space inside was taken up by fuel. An ordinary car could drive around the world about 400 times with that much fuel.

Three hours after liftoff, the rocket separated and fell back to Earth.

It took three days for an Apollo spacecraft to travel to the moon. Two astronauts flew the LM down to the moon's surface while the third astronaut orbited the moon in the CM.

To leave the moon, the top half of the LM blasted off, using the bottom half as a launch-pad. The bottom half of the LM remained on the moon and the top linked up with the CM. After the astronauts entered the CM, the LM was cut loose.

The CM was the only section that could make it back to Earth. On entering Earth's atmosphere, parachutes opened to slow its rapid fall before a splash-landing in the sea. The crew was picked up by waiting ships.

In four years, 27 Apollo astronauts went to the moon and 12 walked on its surface. Because there is no air, water, or weather on the moon, the footprints and the American flags they left there may last for a million years.

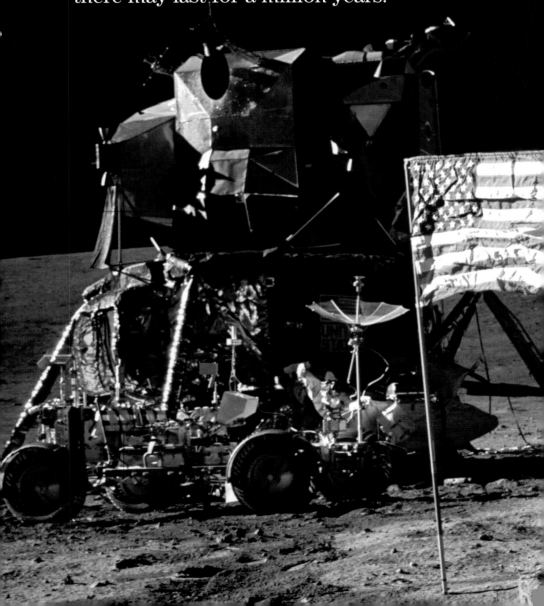

The Apollo missions showed that astronauts could work on the moon in only one-sixth of the gravity of Earth. The six missions that landed on the moon brought back 880 pounds of lunar rocks and a wealth of information about the moon. But because human space travel is so expensive and dangerous, only unmanned spaceships to the planets have been used since the Apollo missions.

A space shuttle is a spacecraft made to be used many times. The first, called Columbia, was launched in 1981. At liftoff, the shuttle weighs 4.5 million pounds, about the weight of 2,000 elephants.

After launch, the boosters' parachutes open and they fall safely back into the ocean where they are picked up to be used again. The fuel tank drops off and breaks up in the atmosphere. Meanwhile, the orbiter travels around Earth at four to five miles per second. At the end of the mission, it re-enters the atmosphere, reaching temperatures of 2,300° Fahrenheit (F).

The orbiter lands like an airplane at about 200 miles per hour, then opens a parachute at its rear to help it slow down.

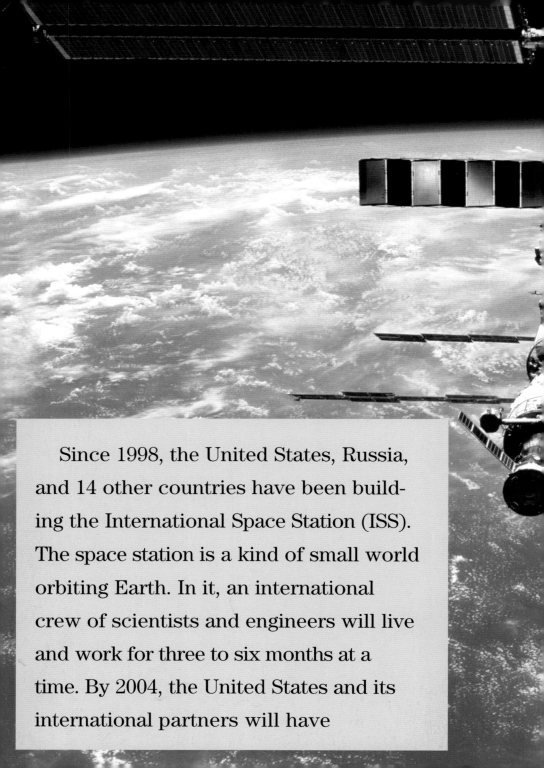

Since 1998, the United States, Russia, and 14 other countries have been building the International Space Station (ISS). The space station is a kind of small world orbiting Earth. In it, an international crew of scientists and engineers will live and work for three to six months at a time. By 2004, the United States and its international partners will have

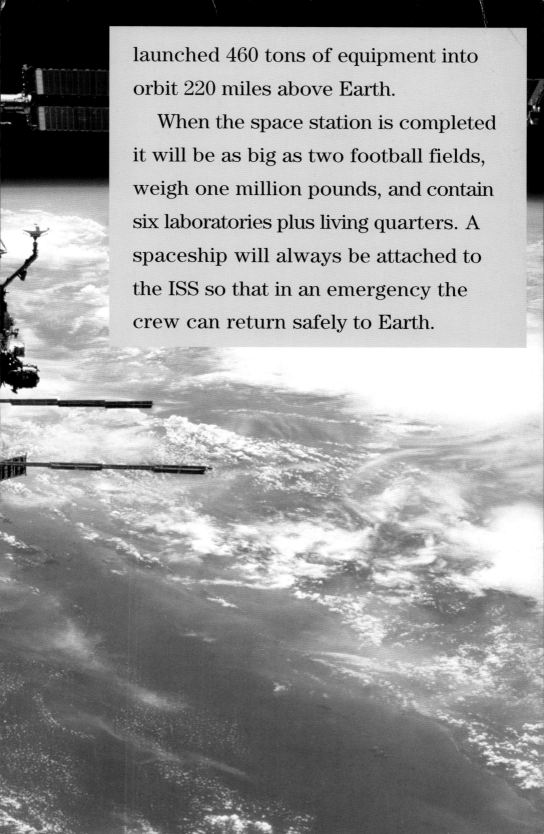

launched 460 tons of equipment into orbit 220 miles above Earth.

When the space station is completed it will be as big as two football fields, weigh one million pounds, and contain six laboratories plus living quarters. A spaceship will always be attached to the ISS so that in an emergency the crew can return safely to Earth.

Though many people want to become astronauts, only a few dozen are chosen for training. They need to know as much as a scientist and be as fit as an athlete. They are trained to use space suits, parachute jump, and survive emergency landings. The astronaut pilots also learn how to fly the shuttle.

Trainees experience low gravity aboard a jet known as the vomit comet. The plane flies to 35,000 feet and then falls 10,000 feet in a steep dive. For 20 to 30 seconds, the astronauts experience weightlessness and float around the cabin. The plane repeats the dive as many as 40 times a day.

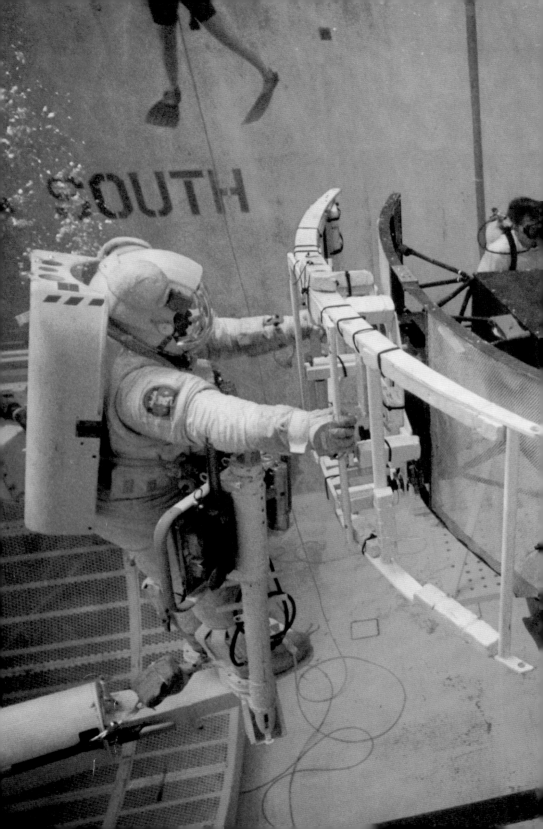

Another training exercise takes place in a huge water tank called the Weightless Environment Training Facility (WETF). The tank contains a life-size reproduction of the shuttle's orbiter bay or other space facilities. Astronauts wear special suits that neither float nor sink in the water. The suits allow them to practice doing tasks in the weightlessness that they will experience in space.

If human beings tried to live in the vacuum of space without protection, they would explode. Space suits provide the protection people need and the oxygen they must breathe. They also help to keep people warm in space, where the temperature is known as absolute zero, or -459° F.

Astronauts wear different suits for launch, for work outside the spacecraft, and for their return to Earth. Inside the shuttle or space station, they wear everyday clothing such as T-shirts and shorts or jogging pants.

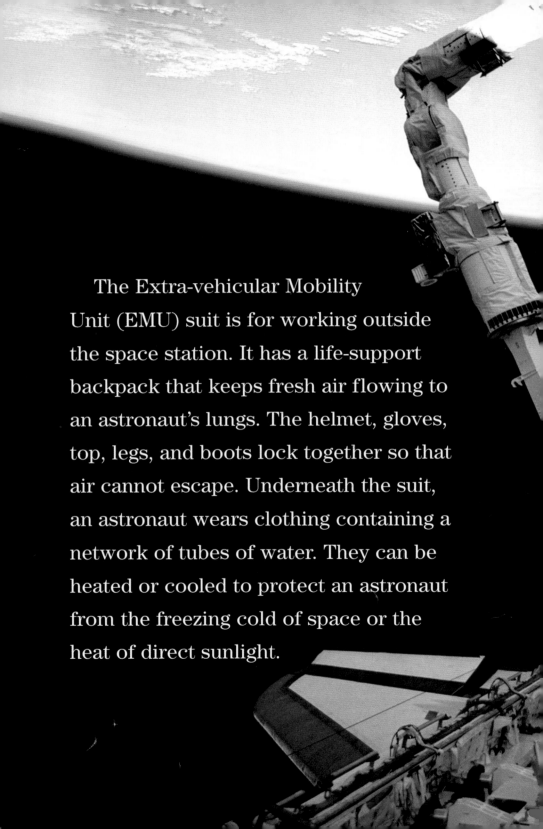

The Extra-vehicular Mobility Unit (EMU) suit is for working outside the space station. It has a life-support backpack that keeps fresh air flowing to an astronaut's lungs. The helmet, gloves, top, legs, and boots lock together so that air cannot escape. Underneath the suit, an astronaut wears clothing containing a network of tubes of water. They can be heated or cooled to protect an astronaut from the freezing cold of space or the heat of direct sunlight.

Astronauts in space have to breathe, sleep, exercise, eat, and use a toilet just like people on Earth. But because they are in a weightless environment, much is done differently.

The astronauts need a constant supply of fresh oxygen, so air has to be recycled. Water vapor from their breath is collected and recycled for drinking. Sleeping bags are tied in place so that the astronauts don't float when sleeping.

Drinks are sucked through tubes so drops of liquid don't float around. Food trays attach to a crew member's legs with straps. Despite the low gravity, most foods stick to ordinary spoons and forks. But if an astronaut drops a knife or fork, it floats about the cabin!

Astronauts even have a toilet that uses air rather than liquid to flush away wastes. Wet wipes are used to clean their bodies afterward.

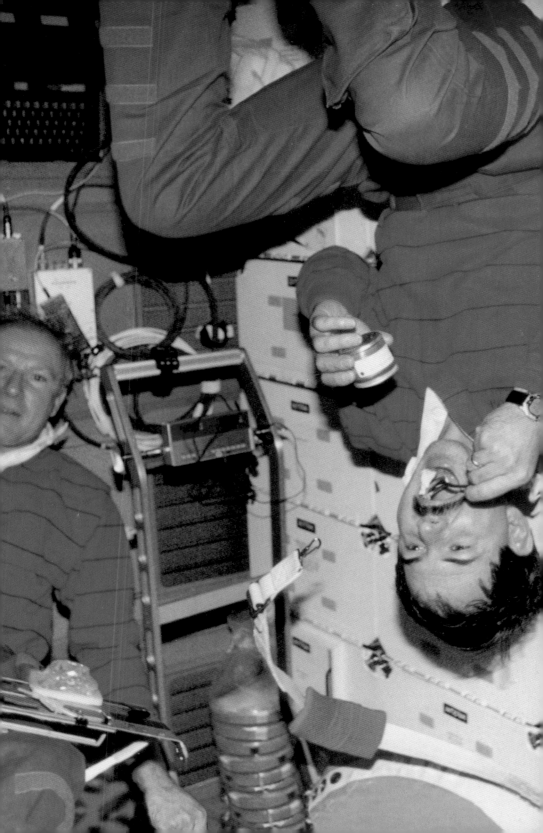

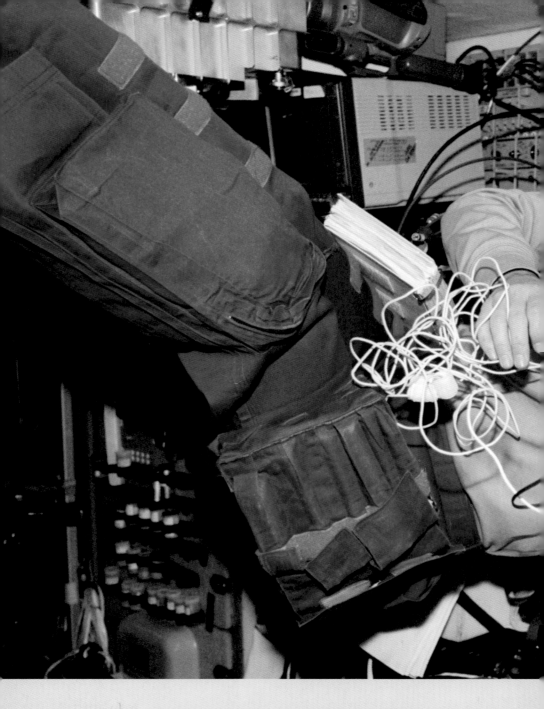

Each day in space is full of carefully planned activities for astronauts, whether they are doing experiments, eating, or exercising. They study

how humans can live in space for long periods of
time. They investigate the effects of weightlessness on people, animals, plants, and equipment.

Extra Vehicular Activity (EVA) is work outside the spacecraft, such as building the space station, fixing problems, or doing experiments. Astronauts on an EVA need to be tied to the spacecraft by a strong rope. They may also wear a Manned Maneuvering Unit (MMU), a jetpack powered by a tank of gas that allows an astronaut to move around the craft.

Tools are not easy to use in the weightlessness of space. Even tightening a screw may need two people—one person to push on the screwdriver, and another to turn it. Otherwise, an astronaut may turn his or her own body rather than the screw!

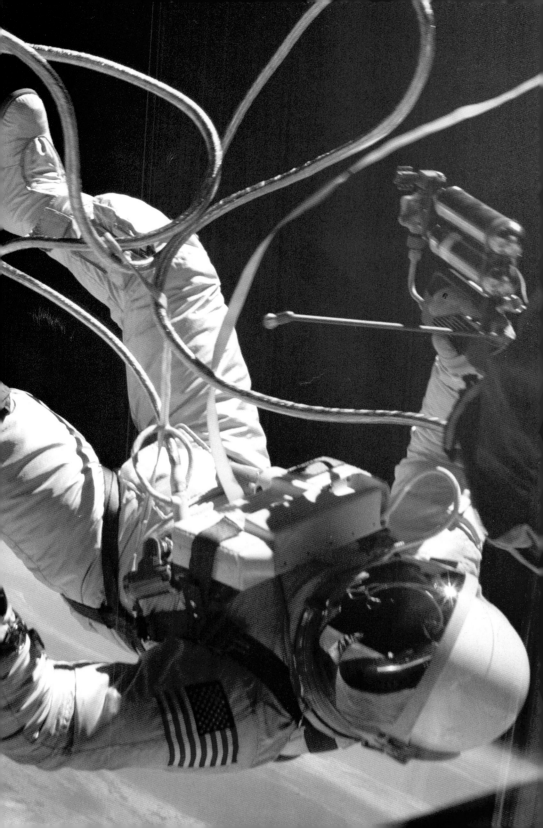

A spacecraft contains hundreds of thousands of parts. The failure of even the smallest part can result in tragedy.

On January 28, 1986, 74 seconds after liftoff, the shuttle Challenger exploded, taking the lives of all seven crew members. Seventeen years later, on February 1, 2003, another terrible accident happened. The shuttle Columbia broke apart and burned as it was descending from orbit, again taking the lives of all seven crew members.

Scientists in the space program try to figure out the causes of accidents and make sure that they don't happen again. Disasters are rare, but they remind us once again of the dangers of space and the bravery of space travelers.

A satellite is any object that orbits around a larger object in space. The moon is Earth's only natural satellite, but more than 1,000 tiny man-made satellites have been sent into its orbit.

Communication satellites beam television pictures, telephone, and computer messages all over the world. Weather satellites watch for storms and changing temperatures of the air, land, and sea. Global positioning satellites can tell people exactly where they are. One of the most famous satellites, the Hubble Space Telescope, has even taken pictures that are almost at the very end of the universe.

Humans have visited the moon, but small robot space probes have gone even farther. Ranging in size from a car to a lunch box, these probes have visited every planet in our solar system except Pluto. They have also taken close looks at the sun, planetary moons, asteroids, and comets.

Pioneer 10 was launched in 1972, more than 30 years ago. It flew by Jupiter in 1973 and began its journey to the stars. The Pioneer's weak signal continues to be tracked from Earth. It is traveling over 25,000 miles an hour toward the red star Aldebaran. That's seven miles per second! Even at that speed, it will take Pioneer 10 over two million years to reach the star.

Perhaps the most famous of all space probes is Voyager 2. Launched into space in 1977, it was supposed to last for five years and visit two planets, Jupiter and Saturn. But against all odds, the 10-foot-tall probe continued on to Uranus and Neptune. It is still traveling outward to the stars. Aboard Voyager is a greeting to the universe—a gold-plated record containing

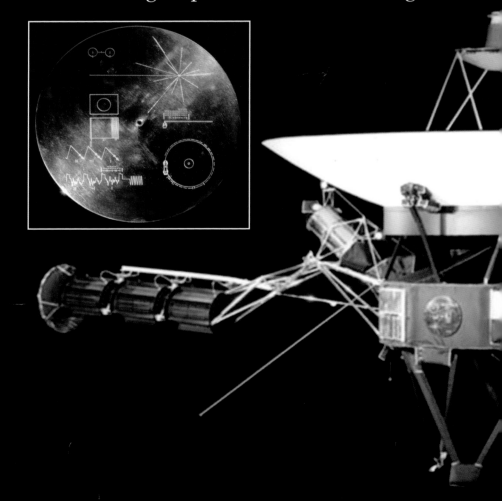

messages in 56 Earth languages along with the sounds of life on our planet.

Some space probes go into orbit around a distant world. Some plunge through its atmosphere or even land on its surface. Space probes have passed through the atmospheres of Venus and Jupiter and made many unexpected discoveries about our solar system.

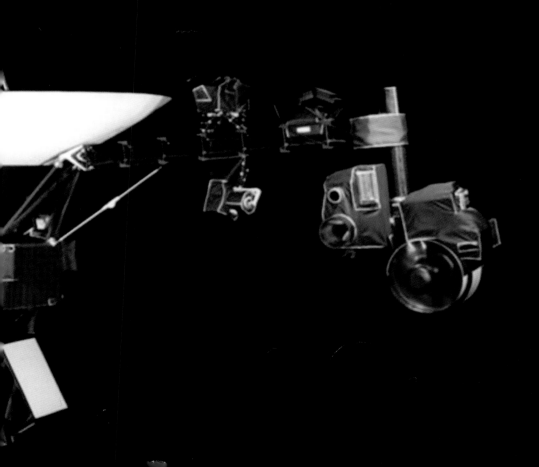

On July 4, 1997, the Mars Pathfinder Lander and its tiny robot rover Sojourner landed on Mars. Since the landing, they have sent more than 17,000 images of the planet.

Pathfinder has examined the chemicals, rocks, and soil on the surface of Mars and has gathered facts about its weather. This information has led scientists to believe that long ago Mars was warm, wet, and had a thicker atmosphere. If water once flowed over the surface of Mars, there is a real possibility that life may once have existed there.

we live at the dawn of the space age. In years to come, astronauts may return to the moon and visit the closer planets. Perhaps one day, people may even live in space stations, on the moon, or even on Mars. As Neil Armstrong said when he became the first human to set foot on the moon, "That's one small step for a man, one giant leap for mankind."